Little **BIG**

JONATHAN BENTLEY

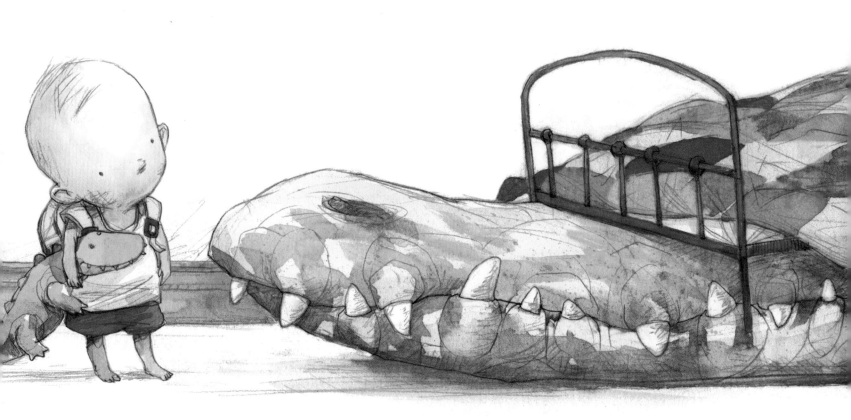

LITTLE HARE
www.littleharebooks.com

I am little.

I try to be **big**.

But it never works.

Little.
Little legs,
little hands,
little mouth.

If I had **big legs** like a giraffe,
I could race my brother up the hill ...
and win.

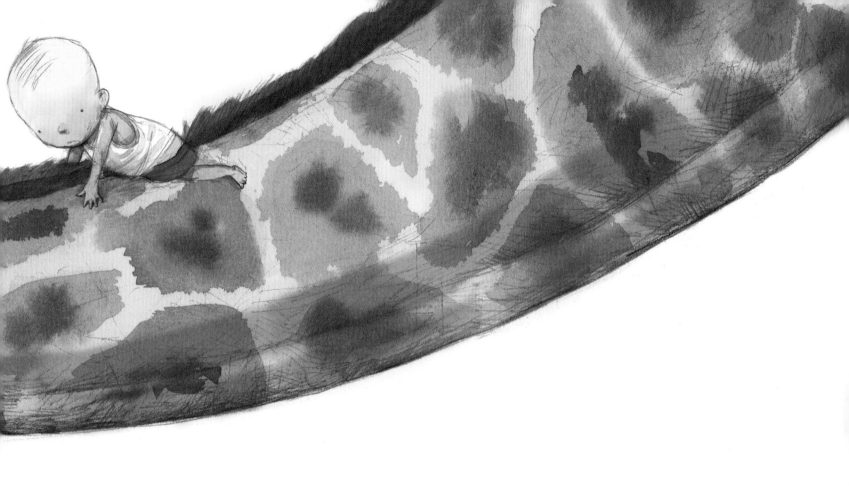

But I wouldn't be able to ride in the trailer.

If I had **big hands** like a gorilla,
I could open the cookie jar

and take as many cookies
as I wanted.

But I wouldn't be able to eat
them in my playhouse.

If I had a **big mouth** like a crocodile,

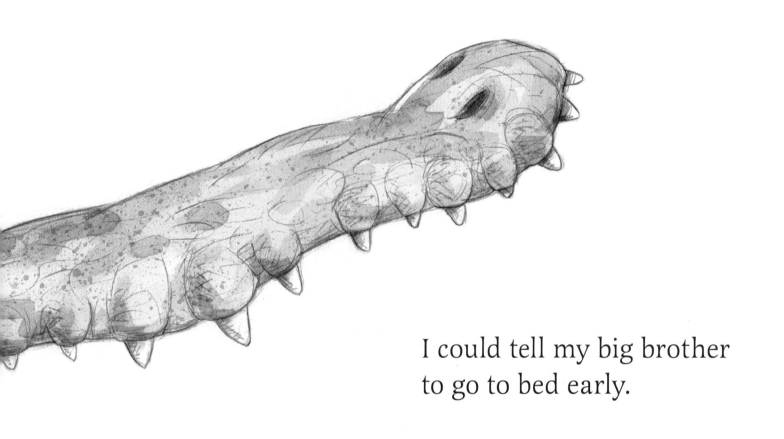

I could tell my big brother
to go to bed early.

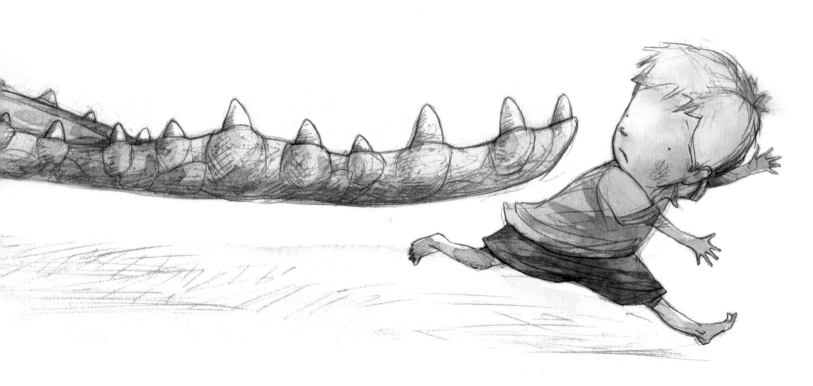

But who would tell me funny stories after dinner?

If I was **big** like a **monster**, I could ...

Run, run, run, little legs.

Hold on tight, little hands.

Not a sound, little mouth.

I am little.

Little legs, little hands, little mouth.

Perfectly little.

For my family — JB

Little Hare Books
an imprint of
Hardie Grant Egmont
Ground Floor, Building 1, 658 Church Street
Richmond, Victoria 3121, Australia

www.littleharebooks.com

First published 2013
First published in paperback 2013

Cataloguing-in-Publication details are available
from the National Library of Australia

978 1 742977 30 0 (pbk.)

Designed by Hannah Robinson, Xou Creative
Produced by Pica Digital, Singapore
Printed through Asia Pacific Offset
Printed in Shenzhen, Guangdong Province, China

5 4 3 2 1

The illustrations in this book were created using watercolours, pencil and scanned textures.